Sensing Peace

Suzana E. Yoder

Illustrated by Rachel Hoffman-Bayles

Herald Press

Scottdale, Pennsylvania
Waterloo, Ontario

Library of Congress Cataloging-in-Publication Data

Yoder, Suzana E., 1984-
  Sensing peace / Suzana E. Yoder ; illustrated by Rachel Hoffman-Bayles.
    p. cm.
  ISBN 978-0-8361-9515-6 (pbk. : alk. paper)
  1. Peace–Juvenile literature. I. Title.
  JZ5538.Y63   2010
  303.6'6–dc22
                             2010007345

SENSING PEACE

Library of Congress Control Number: 2010007345
International Standard Book Number: 978-0-8361-9515-6

15 14 13 12 11 10   10 9 8 7 6 5 4 3 2 1

To order or request information please call 1-800-245-7894 or visit www.heraldpress.com.

Author Dedication
To the children of Philadelphia,
with the belief and prayer that you *can* be peace.
And to Kyle, for all your love and encouragement.

Illustrator Dedication
For Audrey, Warner, Joseph, and Nathan, my little
peacemakers, and for Dallyn, the love of my life.

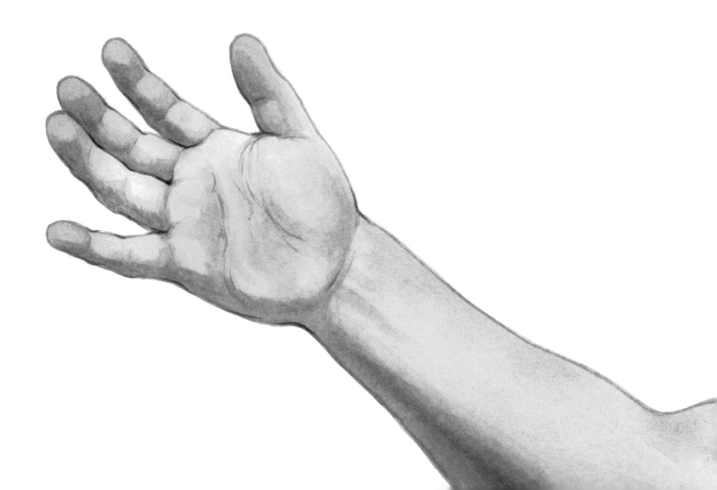

What does peace *look* like? Can you *see* peace?

Peace looks like being a friend to everyone. Peace looks like girls and boys all over the world getting the chance to learn and play in schools.

Peace looks like neighbors sharing their time and sharing their belongings, sharing cars and sharing food. Peace looks like kindness.

You can see peace when friends clean up their neighborhood together. Peace looks like picking up trash and raking leaves. Peace looks like a newly planted tree with branches reaching out and up to the sky. Peace looks like caring for the earth. Look for peace!

What does peace *sound* like? Can you *hear* peace?
You can hear peace in the sweet laughter of your family at
dinnertime. You hear peace in the sound of a familiar voice
on the phone—your best friend, your Grandpop, or your
cousin calling from far away.

Peace sounds joyful and boisterous when children fill the park with happy squeals of play. Peace sounds like a great commotion when people everywhere are talking, singing, and laughing.

Peace can also sound quiet and still. Peace sounds like listening. Peace can be heard in singing birds and chirping crickets. You can hear the cool, calm voice of peace as wind rustles through leaves. Peace sounds like a favorite bedtime story softly told each night.

Peace sounds like the whole world singing a lullaby . . . all the people and all the earth in beautiful harmony. Be still. Listen for peace!

Can you *taste* peace? Peace tastes pure and refreshing—like cool, clean water for everyone around the world to drink.

Peace tastes like the freshly baked cookies you brought to school to share. Imagine sharing an ice-cream sundae with the whole world. That's how peace would taste!

Peace tastes like trying new foods—flatbread with spicy dhal from India, long Chinese noodles, sweet fried plantains from Guatemala, a bowl of sweet and sticky rice from Thailand, Mexican tortillas with beans, and pizza too. (From Italy, you know!)

Welcome others. Share food and taste peace!

Surely you can't *smell* peace, right?
Take a deep, deep breath. Can you smell peace?
Peace is the delightful aroma that fills Grandmom's
kitchen and welcomes everyone in.

Peace is the smell of summer barbecues
and picnics, block parties and neighborhood
gatherings wafting through the street—
bidding all neighbors to come,
eat, share, and be together.

Peace is the smell of campfire smoke
swirling upward to night's starry sky.
It's the scent of ocean air carried toward
you by the wind, so salty you can taste it.

Peace is the smell of earth on your hands after planting a garden.
You can smell peace after a summer rain. Breathe deeply.
Breathe in peace!

What does peace *feel* like?
Can you touch peace?

Peace is feeling summer grass between your toes and crunchy autumn leaves beneath your shoes. Peace is snowflakes falling softly around you and friends dashing quickly through springtime showers. Peace feels like napping in the sunshine. It feels like hugs and high-fives.

Peace is the feeling of having a safe place to live and a warm place to rest. Peace feels like everyone having enough, no one too little and no one too much. Peace is the feeling of full tummies for all the world's children.

You touch peace when you touch the earth, when you hold a hand, when you wipe away tears. Reach out. Touch peace!

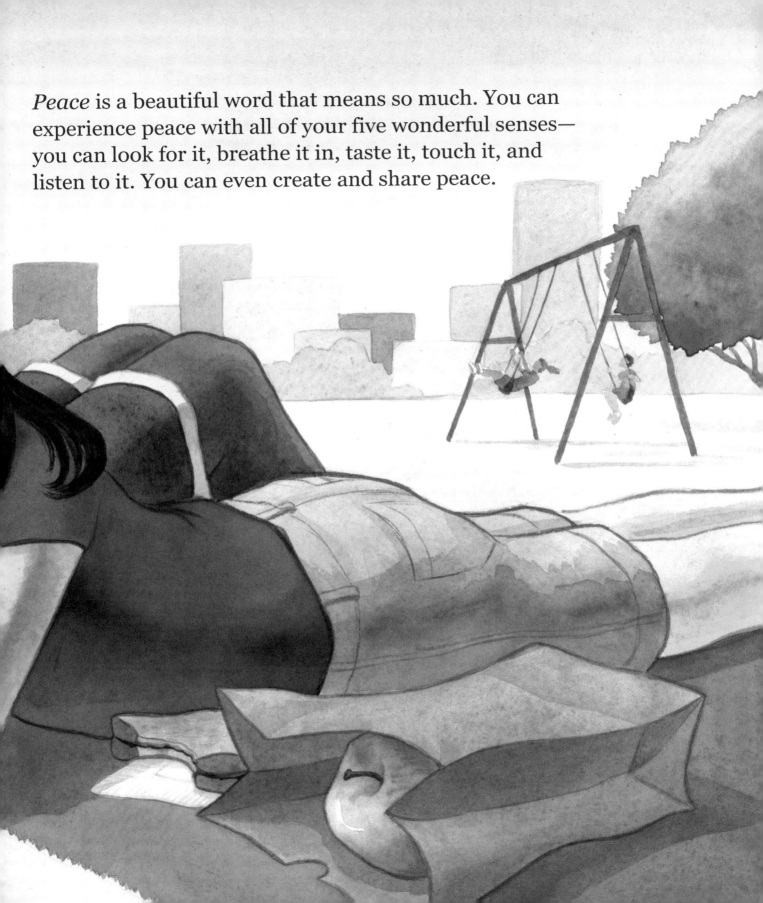

Peace is a beautiful word that means so much. You can experience peace with all of your five wonderful senses— you can look for it, breathe it in, taste it, touch it, and listen to it. You can even create and share peace.

But best of all you can choose to *be* peace. You can *be* peace to the earth as you walk gently and kindly. You can *be* peace to others as you play, learn, and choose to be a friend. You can be kind and generous. You can be compassionate and caring.

Touch, taste, breathe, listen, and look for peace.
Create and share peace. Choose to be peace!

Suzana E. Yoder is a teacher committed to inspiring students to act for peace. She believes that children can learn to live out peace in small but meaningful ways. When she was a kindergarten teacher in Philadelphia, Suzana experienced the way young children are able to understand and conceptualize peace and justice. She strives to nurture and encourage this spirit of peacemaking while working with students.

Suzana grew up in Souderton, Pennsylvania, where she attended Christopher Dock Mennonite High School (Lansdale, Pa.) and went on to graduate from Goshen (Indiana) College. She majored in elementary education and moved to Philadelphia shortly after graduating to teach in an urban setting.

Suzana is currently pursuing a master's degree in special education as an intervention specialist for grades kindergarten to twelve. She also serves as a court-appointed advocate on the behalf of abused and neglected children. Suzana and her husband, Kyle, are members of West Philadelphia Mennonite Fellowship.

Rachel Hoffman-Bayles was raised near Dallas and received a Bachelor of Fine Arts in illustration from Brigham Young University in Provo, Utah. After graduating, she worked as an in-house artist and animator for both Imagine Learning and Waterford Institute, and as a web designer for Equifax.

Now a full-time mother of four children, Rachel continues to work as a freelance illustrator and designer as her busy life permits. She also finds time to publish a line of Christmas cards through her company, Lady Rachel's Garden.

Rachel's other interests include cooking, gardening, reading, writing, traveling, acting, and singing, especially with her professional singer-actor husband, Dallyn. She resides in the New York City area and is an active member of The Church of Jesus Christ of Latter-day Saints.